THE PICKLE JAR

WestBow Press books may be ordered through booksellers or by contacting:

WestBow Press
A Division of Thomas Nelson & Zondervan
1663 Liberty Drive
Bloomington, IN 47403
www.westbowpress.com
844-714-3454

ISBN: 978-1-6642-4830-4 (sc)
ISBN: 978-1-6642-4832-8 (hc)
ISBN: 978-1-6642-4831-1 (e)

Library of Congress Control Number: 2021921959

Print information available on the last page.

WestBow Press rev. date: 11/04/2021

DEDICATED TO

The people that inspire me and truly are my **treasures**!

I LOVE YOU

Mr. T

Sally

Jeff

Veronica

Robert

my grandsons:

Tyler

Trevor

Trenton

(a.k.a. Jerry, Joey & Little Jack)

ACKNOWLEDGEMENT

♥♥♥♥♥♥

To my Lord and Savior, Jesus Christ, who helps me accomplish what He puts in my heart!

THE PICKLE JAR

Connie B. Drumm

"Let it rain, let it rain!" thought Aunt Nellie. Mud puddles were forming everywhere, and the rain was flooding the toy trucks that were scattered on the porch.

Aunt Nellie stood by the front door with Goober, her old wiener dog, while waiting for the excitement to begin. It would only be minutes before nephews Jerry, Joey, and little Jack would arrive for a weekend visit! Aunt Nellie was worried that the rain would spoil the planned adventures but was reminded these boys were full of fun and a little rain would not change a thing, except give them more frogs to catch. She could see the packed car bouncing down the narrow muddy road getting closer and closer! Aunt Nellie started waving and Goober's tail began wagging!

All of a sudden their sliding car came to a stop, barely missing Aunt Nellie's favorite rose bush!

FROG TOWN

Out jumped three eager boys, all wanting to be the first to hug their special aunt!

“I got here first Aunt Nellie,” shouted Jerry, the oldest and determined to be the winner.

“No, you didn’t. I beat you,” added Joey, with one hand holding onto the bottom of Aunt Nellie’s big bulky sweater!

“What about me? I want a hug too,” frowned little Jack, just as they all tumbled on to the floor, laughing and rolling on top of each other.

Mom and dad’s last words could be heard ... “You boys be good. Mind your Aunt Nellie and not too many popsicles and cookies!”

It did not take long to get their back packs emptied and settled into their favorite spots, while Aunt Nellie fixed a batch of cookies and put more wood on the fire. The home felt so cozy and warm. The boys wanted to stay with their aunt forever!

“WOW look outside! It is raining so hard. I can even hear it hit the porch,” said Joey. Little Jack joined Joey at the kitchen window to watch the rain. The leaves were flying everywhere, and the strong winds were bending the tree branches. Little Jack tried counting the rain drops as they sled down the window, while Joey watched frogs play in mud puddles.

“Let the fun begin!” said Jerry. Aunt Nellie sat down with a loaded plate of yummy chocolate chip cookies as everyone snuggled together by the fireplace laughing and telling knock-knock jokes!

“I have an idea,” said Aunt Nellie. “Let’s tell stories. Who wants to be first? Aunt Nellie always came up with fun things to do.

“You start Auntie. We want you,” begged Joey.

“Okay,” she said, “You win!”

Knock-knock.
Who's there?

And then her story began ... "Well, this happened a long time ago, but I still think about it every day. I used to teach a Sunday School class to kids just about your age."

"My age?" asked Jerry.

"No, probably Joey's age, around 7."

"Cool," smiled Joey, feeling super special.

"I loved that class!!! We talked about Jesus and how much He loves all the children of the world. We had a fun time. I always ended Sunday School in prayer and told the kids "I love you and Jesus loves you more." They would smile, hug me, throw me a kiss, or show me a thumbs up, EXCEPT JENNY!" She was different, but that was okay. Jenny would be the first one in class and sat in the back, all by herself. She looked sad, never smiled or talked with the other kids. It broke my heart."

"I would have been her friend," whispered Joey, with sniffles and tears coming down his sweet face.

"And a good friend too!" added Aunt Nellie.

Outside the thunder was roaring so loud the boys started to get restless and nervous. Goober jumped on little Jack's lap and started shaking. Aunt Nellie stood up and cheerfully said, "I think it's time for a group hug!" That's exactly what they needed.

"Whatever happened to that girl?" asked Joey. Aunt Nellie became quiet. It was hard to continue. "Well, Jenny stopped coming to Sunday School. I don't know why and thought I would never see her again!"

Jerry left the room and yelled back, "Aunt Nellie, hold on!" He returned with a box of tissue and started drying her tears, as she softly patted his hand. Aunt Nellie continued sharing her story.

"Then one Sunday as I was leaving class, I looked up and noticed a child standing in the doorway. Could it be Jenny, I thought? We stared at each other for a few minutes and suddenly she ran to me and hugged me real tight. I felt her tears against my dress. She looked up at me and smiled with a dirty face that was so beautiful. Jenny took my hand and kissed it, as she placed a heart shaped piece of paper inside. I remember her wearing blue mittens that barely covered her cold hands as she turned to leave."

"That makes me sad," said little Jack. "It's not fun being cold, especially if you are alone!"

"That is so true little Jack."

"Then as she was leaving, she looked back at me with the biggest smile and gave me a thumbs up! At that moment I opened my hand and written on the heart-shaped piece of paper were these words, "*I love you Miss Nellie and Jesus loves you more, Love Jenny,*" I knew then that Jenny would be okay."

The boys stretched and finished their cookies. "Aunt Nellie, what happened to the heart Jenny gave you. Can we see it?" asked Jerry.

Aunt Nellie hung her head saying, *"I don't know. It could be anywhere or gone forever!"*

The boys didn't know what to say to help Aunt Nellie feel better. But they did notice the rain had stopped!

"Hey, Aunt Nellie, do you have any jars we can use for our frogs and worms?" Jerry was anxious to get outside.

"Look in the old shed near the back porch. It is an awful mess. BE CAREFUL!"

Jerry peeked in the window. "Oh WOW," he thought, "It is a huge mess." It was full of stacked boxes. The door squeaked as he stepped inside. He saw an old rusty wagon with three wheels, a cracked fishbowl, and several smelly boots, but mostly boxes of broken jars filled with dead flies and gross bugs.

Jerry felt disappointed and started to leave. Then he stopped! Right in front of him he saw the perfect size jar, and he went to grab it! He jumped and screamed as a big fat rat jumped to the floor and ran behind the stacked boxes. Jerry was out the door fast!

"Hey guys, I found a jar and a huge ugly rat found me!"

"You silly boys," said Aunt Nellie. Joey and little Jack started laughing and teasing Jerry. Aunt Nellie looked at the jar and her heart started pounding faster and faster!!

"Wait!" As she rubbed the dirt off the jar and looked inside, her eyes filled up with tears. She could barely speak. "This is it boys. You found it. This is THE PICKLE JAR!"

PICKLES

The house was so full of joy Aunt Nellie started singing "Thank you Jesus," and hugging each boy so tight!

Little Jack wondered, "What is so special about a pickle jar? Aunt Nellie, can we have another popsicle?"

They all gathered around the kitchen table and Aunt Nellie emptied the jar. Their eyes questioned what they saw. Joey pointed to the shiny seashells.

"Where did these come from, Aunt Nellie?"

Aunt Nellie handed him one and replied, "Remember when we made sandcastles on the beach? You put these in my hand, kissed me on my cheek, and said I love you Auntie."

"I did? That was a long time ago." Aunt Nellie held his face in her warm hands and said, "You made me feel so special!" Joey blushed and smiled.

"Look at those awesome rocks. Where did these come from?" asked little Jack. He wanted to hold the big one.

"Jerry, remember when we walked to the park for a picnic? Before we even got there you started collecting rocks and filling up your pockets. When we got home you lined them up on a bench and started painting. "I" on the first rock, "Love" on the second rock, and "You" on the third rock, and saved the others. I found them when I went to bed. You had laid them on my pillow. You made me feel so special!"

"Because you are special Aunt Nellie." Jerry laid his head on her soft shoulder and tickled her chin. Aunt Nellie giggled and winked at him.

"Hey, what about me? Don't forget me!" Little Jack wiggled in and sat on Aunt Nellie's lap.

"Did I give you anything?" Aunt Nellie gently picked up the fragile pieces of flowers that laid close by.

"Little Jack, I saved these for a long time. You were just a little guy and loved digging in the dirt. After I planted some beautiful daisies in my garden, you decided to pick all of them and came running to me with a beautiful bouquet. You looked up at me with those big brown eyes and said, "I love you Auntie!" You were covered in dirt. All I could think about was hugging you."

Little Jack mumbled, "Sorry I got you dirty!"

"I wasn't worried about any dirt. I cherish that moment because you made me feel so special!"

Little Jack was embarrassed and bent over and kissed Goober! Goober thought he was getting something to eat!

LOVE
YOU
HOLY BIBLE
HOLY BIBLE

“These are all treasures in my pickle jar. They remind me how special and loved you each made me feel.”

Aunt Nellie wanted them to know that their actions of thoughtfulness were a gift of love! Jesus wants us to be thoughtful and caring of each other. So many people have never heard ... *I love you; Jesus loves you, or you are special!*

After the boys finished their last popsicle, Aunt Nellie tucked them in their beds by the warm fireplace. Before they could finish their individual prayers, they were all fast asleep. Even old Goober!

Dear Jesus...

Morning came and mom and dad arrived to pick them up. With backpacks on and worms in their pockets, they stopped on the porch for one more group hug! Aunt Nellie handed each of them their very own pickle jar, as she kissed them one last time. They were excited!! Inside their jars was a *SURPRISE!*

Aunt Nellie made three crosses from the leftover popsicle sticks. One cross was put in each jar as a reminder that she loves them, they are special to her and Jesus loves them too. This would be their first treasure in their own pickle jar.

As the car drove off, Aunt Nellie slowly walked inside, missing the boys already! On the kitchen table she saw a little folded piece of paper sitting on top of her Bible. "Maybe the boys forgot it," she thought. She unfolded it and her eyes filled up with happy tears. It was a big red heart with these words, *"We love you so much Aunt Nellie, and Jesus loves you more, Love, Jerry, Joey, and little Jack!"*

But wait, she noticed something else! She picked up the pickle jar and could see something stuck to the side, near the bottom of the jar. She gently reached in and took it out. It was old, torn, and faded. It was heart shaped. She knew what it was and smiled as tears slowly dropped on two words ... *Love Jenny*! Aunt Nellie felt so loved and special! She picked up the folded heart from the boys and put both treasures where they belonged ... in **THE PICKLE JAR!**

The End

Author Biography

Connie B. Drumm was born and raised in a Christian home in Oakland, CA. She graduated in 1975 from L.I.F.E Bible College, Los Angeles, CA (currently Life Pacific University, San Dimas, CA). As a licensed-ordained minister with the International Church of the Foursquare Gospel. She served as Children's & Youth Minister for many years at Hayward Foursquare church (currently New Hope Christian Fellowship). She feels blessed with a loving Christian family, Tom Drumm, her husband of 13 years, son, Jeff Price and wife, Veronica, daughter, Sally Price, and three grandsons, 14 yr. old Tyler, 8 yr. old Trevor, and 5 yr. old Trenton. She retired from Department of Homeland Security TSA & FPS in 2015. She is a Breast Cancer Survivor since 2016! Praise God! Her interests include creative writing, photography, interior decorating, camping, and spending "Grammy Days" with her grandsons. She and her husband, Tom, now live in Oakdale, CA (Cowboy Capital of the World)."THE PICKLE JAR" is her 3rd children's book with a beautiful Christian message.

Printed in the United States
by Baker & Taylor Publisher Services